P9-BZH-390
SOUTH SAN FRANCISCO PUBLIC LIBRARY

The Crane Wife

Retold by SUMIKO YAGAWA
Translation from the Japanese by KATHERINE PATERSON
Illustrated by SUEKICHI AKABA

William Morrow and Company New York 1981

In a faraway mountain village, where the snow falls deep and white, there once lived all alone a poor young peasant named Yohei. One day, at the beginning of winter, Yohei went out into the snow to run an errand, and, as he hurried home, suddenly *basabasa* he heard a rustling sound. It was a crane, dragging its wing, as it swooped down and landed on the path. Now Yohei could see that the bird was in great pain, for an arrow had pierced its wing. He went to where the crane lay, drew out the arrow, and very carefully tended its wound.

Late that night there came a tapping *hotohoto* on the door of Yohei's hut. It seemed very peculiar for someone to be calling at that time of night. When he slid open the door to look out, there before him stood a beautiful young woman.

"I beg you, sir," she said in a voice both delicate and refined, "please allow me to become your wife."

Yohei could hardly believe his ears. The more closely he looked, the more noble and lovely the woman appeared. Gently he took her hand and brought her inside.

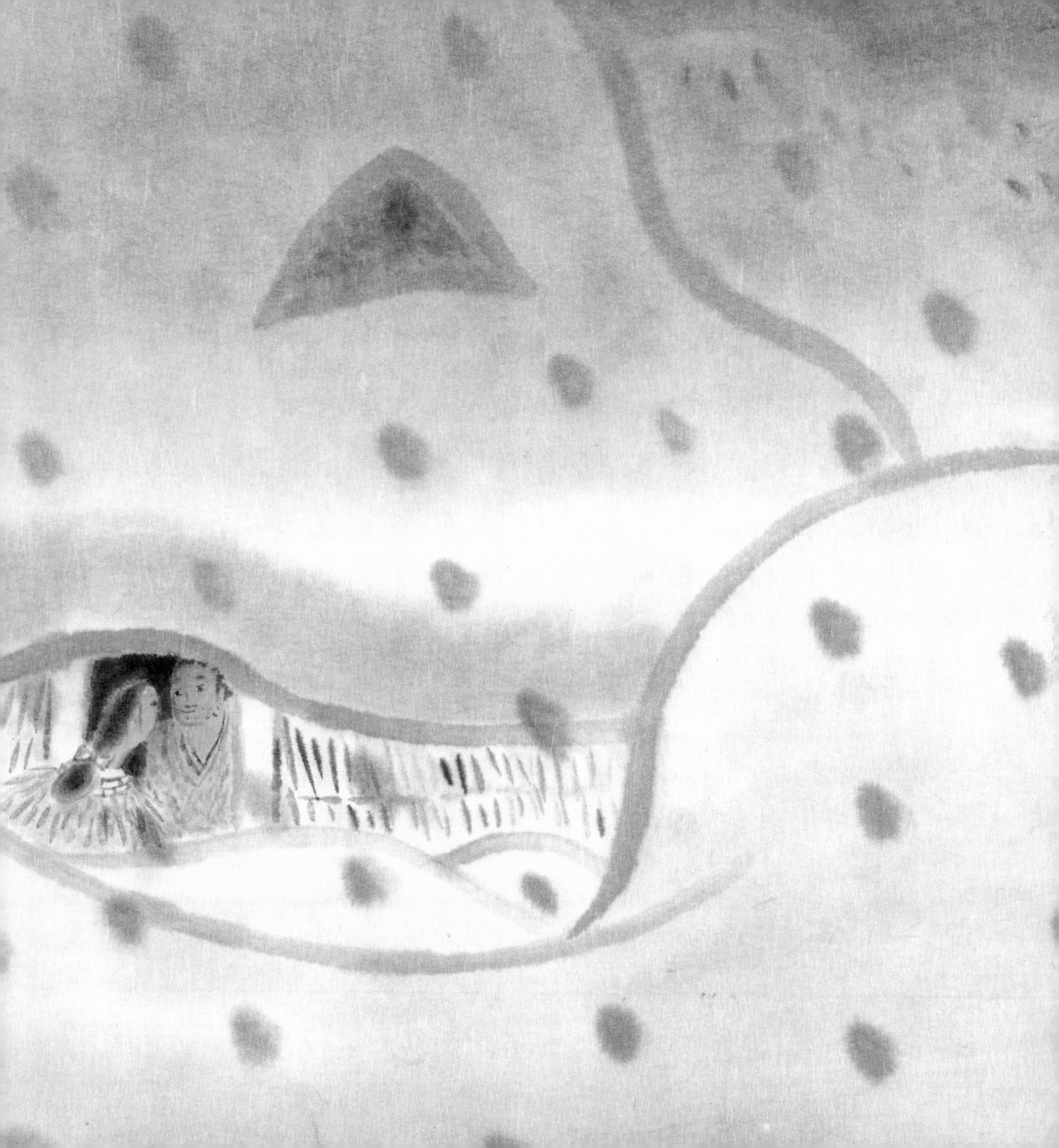

"Yohei has got some fine wife at his house," the villagers gossiped among themselves.

And it was true. The young woman was modest and kind, and she served Yohei faithfully. He could no longer recognize the cold, cold dreary hut where he had lived all alone, his house had become so bright and warm. The simple Yohei was happier than he could have ever dreamed.

In reality, however, with two mouths to feed instead of one, poor Yohei became poorer than he was before. And, since it was winter and there was no work to be found, he was very quickly coming to the bottom of what he had stored away.

At this point the young woman had a suggestion. "The other women of the village have looms upon which to weave cloth," she said. "If you would be so kind as to allow it, I should like to try my hand at weaving too."

In the back room of the hut, the young woman set up a loom and closed it off with sliding paper doors. Then she said to Yohei, "Please, I beg you, I beg you never look in upon me while I am weaving."

Tonkara tonkara. For three days and three nights the sound of the loom continued. Without stopping either to eat or drink, the young woman went on weaving and weaving. Finally, on the fourth day, she came out. To Yohei she seemed strangely thin and completely exhausted as, without a word, she held out to him a bolt of material.

And such exquisite cloth it was! Even Yohei, who had absolutely no knowledge of woven goods, could only stare in astonishment at the elegant, silken fabric.

Yohei took the cloth and set out for town. There he was able to sell it for such a high price that for a while the two of them had enough money to live quite comfortably and pleasantly.

The winter, however, stretched on and on until, finally, there was very little money left. Yohei hesitated to say anything, so he kept quiet, but at last the young woman spoke up. "I shall weave on the loom one more time. But, please, let this be the last." And, once more, having been warned not to look in on the woman as she wove, the simple Yohei settled down to wait outside just as she asked.

This time the weaving took four days and four nights. A second time the young woman appeared carrying a bolt of cloth, but now she seemed thinner and more pathetic than before. The fabric, moreover, was lighter and even more beautiful. It seemed almost to glow with a light all its own.

Yohei sold the material for an even higher price than the first time. "My," he marveled, "what a good wife I have!" The money bag he carried was heavy, but Yohei's heart was light, and he fairly skipped as he hurried home.

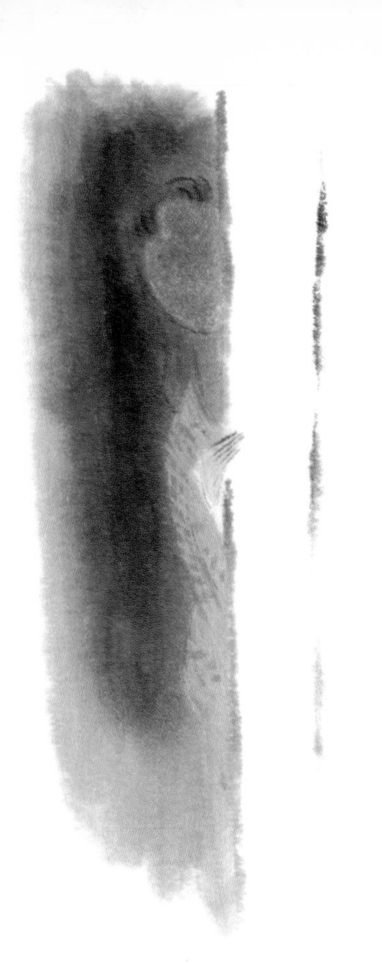

Now the man next door had noticed that Yohei seemed to be living far more grandly than he had in the old days, and he was most curious. Pretending to be very casual about it all, he made his way through the snow and began to chat. Yohei, being a simple and innocent fellow, told the neighbor how his wife's woven goods had brought a wonderful price.

The man became more curious than ever. "Tell me," he said, "just what kind of thread does your wife use? My woman's cotton cloth never fetched a price like that. If your wife's stuff is as marvelous as you say, you ought to take it to the capital, to the home of some noble. You could probably sell it for ten times–for a hundred times more. Say, how about it? Why don't you let me do it for you? We'd split the profits right down the middle. Just think of it! We could live out the rest of our lives doing nothing but sitting back and fanning ourselves."

Before Yohei's very eyes, gold coins great and small began to dazzle and dance. If only he could get his wife to relent, if only he could persuade her to weave again, they could seize such a fortune as had never been known before.

When Yohei presented her with this idea, the young woman seemed quite perplexed. "Why in the world," she asked, "would anyone need so much money as that?"

"Don't you see?" he answered. "With money like that a man's problems would all disappear. He could buy anything he liked. He could even start his own business."

"Isn't it plenty to be able to live together, just the two of us?"

When she spoke this way, Yohei could say no more. However, from that time on, whether asleep or awake, all he could do was think about money. It was so painful for the young woman to see Yohei in this state that her eyes filled with tears as she watched him, until finally, unable to bear it another day, she bowed to his will.

"Very well then," she said. "I will weave one more time. But truly, after this, I must never weave again." And once more she warned the now-joyful Yohei, saying, "For the sake of heaven, remember. Do not look in on me."

Yohei rubbed his hands together in his eagerness and sat down to wait.

Tonkara tonkara. The sound of the loom continued on and on into the fifth day. The work in the back room seemed to be taking longer than ever.

Yohei, no longer the simple fellow that he had once been, began to wonder about certain peculiar things. Why did the young woman appear to grow thinner every time she wove? What was going on in there behind those paper doors? How could she weave such beautiful cloth when she never seemed to buy any thread?

The longer he had to wait, the more he yearned to peep into the room until, at last, he put his hand upon the door.

"Ah!" came a voice from within. At the same time Yohei cried out in horror and fell back from the doorway.

What Yohei saw was not human. It was a crane, smeared with blood, for with its beak it had plucked out its own feathers to place them in the loom.

At the sight Yohei collapsed into a deep faint.

When he came to himself, he found, lying near his hand, a bolt of fabric, pure and radiantly white, through which was woven a thread of bright crimson. It shone with a light this world has never known.

From somewhere Yohei heard the whisper of a delicate, familiar voice. "I had hoped," the voice said sorrowfully, "that you would be able to honor my entreaty. But because you looked upon me in my suffering, I can no longer tarry in the human world. I am the crane that you saved on the snowy path. I fell in love with your gentle, simple heart, and, trusting it alone, I came to live by your side. I pray that your life will be long and that you will always be happy."

"Wai–t!" Yohei stumbled in his haste to get outside.

It was nearly spring, and, over the crest of the distant mountains, he could barely discern the tiny form of a single crane, flying farther and farther away.

Note to the Reader

"The Crane Wife" is perhaps Japan's most loved folktale. It has been made into plays, movies, and even an opera. Every year thousands of Japanese will go to see some version of the story as well as read it or tell it to their children.

The pronunciation of the Japanese words preserved in the text is as follows:

Yohei –Yoh-hay. This name has no particular meaning. It is a typical name for a simple country fellow.

Basabasa –This is an onomatopoeic word to indicate the sound of rustling wings. The *a* is like *ah,* and the word should be read in a sort of whisper so that it sounds like rustling wings.

Hotohoto – Another onomatopoeic word. The *o* is like a short *oh.* Make your mouth round, and you will have a hollow sound of someone tapping on a wooden door.

Tonkara tonkara –This is the sound of the loom at work. Again *o* is *oh,* the *a* is *ah.* The *n* before the *k* has a sort of nasal sound. There is an accent on the *ton* syllable. Thus you have something like: Tohng' kahrah. But say all the vowel sounds briskly to get the effect of a loom.

Tsuru-nyōbō—The Crane Wife
Retold by Sumiko Yagawa copyright © 1979
Illustrated by Suekichi Akaba copyright © 1979
Originally published in Japan in 1979 by Fukuinkan-Shoten, Publishers, Inc., Tokyo.
English translation copyright © 1981 by Katherine Paterson
 Inquiries should be addressed to William Morrow and Company, Inc., 105 Madison Ave., New York, N. Y. 10016. Printed in Japan. 1 2 3 4 5 6 7 8 9 10

Library of Congress Cataloging in Publication Data

Yagawa, Sumiko. The crane wife. Translation of Tsuru-nyōbō.
Summary: After Yohei tends a wounded crane, a beautiful young woman begs to become his wife and three times weaves for him an exquisite silken fabric on her loom.
[1. Folklore–Japan] I. Akaba, Suekichi. II. Title.
PZ8.1.Y25Cr 398.2'1'0952 [E] 80-29278 ISBN 0-688-00496-2 ISBN 0-688-00497-0 (lib. bdg.)